S.M. Ascough describes himself as 'Just an ordinary working man, but with the imagination of a child'. He takes pleasure in the simple things in life such as gardening with his wife or enjoying a trip into the countryside with his family.

Putting his imagination to work, he wanted to write stories with a moral and a message that would make the reader stop and think.

Written in honour of the late Dr Horace Dobbs in the hope that his work will one day be recognised as the first steps to a more harmonious world.

S.M. Ascough

The Dolphin's Message

Austin Macauley Publishers™
LONDON • CAMBRIDGE • NEW YORK • SHARJAH

Copyright © S.M. Ascough 2024

The right of S.M. Ascough to be identified as the author of this work has been asserted by the author in accordance with sections 77 and 78 of the Copyright, Designs and Patents Act 1988.

All rights reserved. No part of this publication may be reproduced, stored in a retrieval system, or transmitted in any form or by any means, electronic, mechanical, photocopying, recording, or otherwise, without the prior permission of the publishers.

Any person who commits any unauthorised act in relation to this publication may be liable to criminal prosecution and civil claims for damages.

This is a work of fiction. Names, characters, businesses, places, events, locales, and incidents are either the products of the author's imagination or used in a fictitious manner. Any resemblance to actual persons, living or dead, or actual events is purely coincidental.

A CIP catalogue record for this title is available from the British Library.

ISBN 9781035838790 (Paperback)
ISBN 9781035838806 (ePub e-book)

www.austinmacauley.com

First Published 2024
Austin Macauley Publishers Ltd®
1 Canada Square
Canary Wharf
London
E14 5AA

It had been another mind-numbing day at the office. Dan slumped down on the seat as the train rattled its way out of the station, past rows of other commuters all looking as numb as he felt.

He stared absently out of the window and watched the low sun reappear as it sank below a cloud, highlighting the contrast of the distant trees with the industrial outskirts of the city. He half-closed his eyes as the late sun's rays pierced the dirty glass of the window.

The carriage momentarily plunged into darkness as they passed through a short tunnel and his view of the sun was replaced by his own reflection.

He looked into his own eyes and started to mentally sing the lyrics of a Queen song, "There must be more to life than this…"

The tunnel ended as suddenly as it came, allowing the sun to brighten the carriage like a spotlight. As his view was restored, he blinked at the contrast from dark to light and his mind wandered further.

"I'm 28 already. And I refuse to become just another anonymous suit that nobody will miss when I'm gone."

"Sorry?" enquired the woman sitting beside him.

Dan realised he must have voiced his thoughts. "I'm sorry, I'm just mumbling. It's been a long day."

She smiled, "Aren't they all?" and returned to her magazine.

Thirty minutes later he stepped off the train and his heart lifted when he saw his wife's car sitting in the car park. She must have finished early, which was a particularly welcome sight as the darkening evening had just turned to rain.

"Am I glad to see you," he said as he leaned across from the passenger seat to kiss her.

Sally smiled. "It just shows how much I love you. The traffic was awful. They've put road works right outside the shop."

"That must be a bit inconvenient."

"Very," she said as she drove onto the main road, flicking the wipers as the rain blurred her vision.

He looked at her as she drove, and he thought, "Maybe life's not as bad as I thought."

Sally was a slim, dark-haired beauty that he fell in love with all those years ago in high school. He always felt that she was too good for him, but it seems that they were meant to be together as neither of them had been in any other relationship.

He put his hand on her knee. "Thanks for coming. I wouldn't have liked walking home in this."

Once they were at home, Dan walked into the room.

"Isn't there a match on?" he asked.

"Oh No. I hope not. I want to watch this," Sally replied, pleading for some consideration.

Dan laughed. "Only kidding."

He sat beside her and put his arm over her shoulder.

"What have you been doing?" Sally asked, her eyes never leaving the screen.

"I've washed up. To say thank you for such a nice meal."

This time her attention moved from the T.V. She looked at him sideways suspiciously. "It was only lasagne."

Dan leaned over and gave a little peck on the cheek. "Thank you."

"Hmph." She turned back to the television.

"So, what's this about?" he asked.

"Whales and dolphins," she replied quietly, trying not to disturb her concentration.

For the next hour, they sat in almost complete silence as they watched divers and cameramen swimming alongside some of the most majestic and gentle creatures of the sea. Their silence was only interrupted by an occasional "Wow" or "Look at that."

As the credits rolled, Sally looked at her husband. "I would love to do that. That has definitely got to go on my bucket list."

"Well, it shouldn't be too difficult. Just arrange it for our next holiday," he offered.

Sally drew her feet up onto the sofa and turned to him. "What? You mean you'd like to do it as well?" she asked.

"Well," he conceded, "it didn't exactly set me on fire, but it would be interesting."

She put her arms around his neck and planted a hard kiss on his lips. "That's fantastic. Are you serious?"

Dan smiled and nodded his assent. "Why not? If it makes you happy."

She hugged him again. "Ooh. Fantastic, fantastic. I'll start looking tomorrow. I'm so excited!"

"Coffee?" he offered. She followed him into the kitchen.

"I once went to a talk about dolphins," he volunteered.

"You never told me."

"Years ago. A Dr Horace Dobbs. He was one of the first to realise how swimming with dolphins could help heal sick kids. He ended up spending the rest of his life studying them. He wrote a couple of books too. I've probably still got them somewhere," he explained.

"I thought you said you weren't interested," she scowled.

Dan joked, "I was more interested in the girl that organised the event," Sally swiftly slapped him on the back of the head.

"Anyway," Dan continued, "after all that walking that we did last year, it will be more relaxing to sit on a boat."

"We can afford it, can't we?"

"Darling. We can afford anything if we want it bad enough. It just means we might have to give up a few other things while we save up."

She hugged him again. "It's no wonder I love you."

Two days later, Dan sat at the breakfast bar watching the clock as he finished his cereal.

Sally poured a coffee. "I've been looking on the internet," she started. "We could go whale watching in Canada, off the Newfoundland coast. It looks beautiful."

"It'll be too cold," he replied. "You wouldn't be doing much swimming." His answer seemed short and definite. "Time to go," he said as he put down his spoon.

Sally looked crestfallen. "You've not changed your mind, have you?" she asked.

"Sorry sweet. Got to go. Can we talk about this tonight?" With a swift kiss on the cheek and without waiting for a reply, he slipped on his coat and left. Sally scowled and set about brushing her hair to vent her frustration.

The day seemed to pass slowly. Work couldn't kept her mind occupied. She rearranged the flowers in the shop window for the third time, but still, her mind wandered, worrying that there was a World Cup or some other footballing event that had distracted him from fulfilling her dream. She so wanted to Google search for more information, but she knew better than to risk her job by using the computer instead of serving customers.

At home that evening, Sally had decided to keep quiet, holding on to her impatience until Dan opened the subject. By eight o'clock they had settled together on the sofa. As she sat, her foot danced as her tension increased. After a further fifteen minutes, Dan seemed more interested in his newspaper. She could wait no longer. Sally had convinced herself that disappointment was only minutes away and the suspense was too much.

"About Canada," she started.

"Oahu," he corrected, trying to hide a smile without looking up from his paper.

"Where?" Sally sat bolt upright as disappointment immediately transformed into hope.

"Oahu," Dan repeated.

"Where Hu? Where's Oahu?" she asked.

Dan put down the paper. "You don't know where Oahu is?"

Sally jumped up, heading to the computer for clarification. Dan was faster, he grabbed her by the hips and pulled her back onto his lap.

"Oahu is one of the Hawaiian Islands," he explained. Her face lit up with delight.

"Surely you've heard of Honolulu?"

"Of course," said Sally indignantly.

"Honolulu is on Oahu. You can surf, snorkel, dance in your grass skirt…" Dan rocked so that Sally wobbled on his knee. "And you'll be able to watch the whales go by while you swim with the dolphins."

Her eyes widened. Dan pulled her close, kissed her gently and then said, "How would you like to go for ten days in the spring?"

Sally could barely contain herself. "Are you serious?" she asked. "Can we afford it?"

Dan smiled and whispered, "I've booked it for April."

Sally exploded. "What? Seriously? You're kidding me! Honestly?"

He smiled widely in triumph, and then shrugged, "Well, I've always wanted to go surfing."

Sally bit her lip. "You really have, haven't you?" she nodded slowly, looking deep into his eyes. "Oh my God, I don't believe it. I love you, I love you, love you, love you."

She threw her arms around him, kissing him again and again. Eventually, she pulled back. "Why April?"

"Because that's when the whales are passing, making their way north. Scores of them. All different species, Humpbacks mostly. Mummies, Daddies, babies – you can't move for them."

"Oh wow! I really don't believe you. You've done research and everything haven't you? There's no wonder I love you so much," she smiled, then paused as a thought distracted her.

"Seven months. I can't wait," she said wistfully. "I wonder if Sandra will let me have the time off."

"I can't see why not. It's after Valentine's Day so you shouldn't be that busy. Anyway, I've arranged it for half-term, so her daughter can help out."

"Great idea," she said. "But I won't tell her it's booked; I'll just ask for the time first."

It was late March. The winter had come and gone, and Christmas was a distant memory.

Sally had been getting busier in a crescendo of activity as the date drew ever closer. Lists were written, scribbled out and rewritten as shopping for bikinis, sarongs, and sandals fuelled her anticipation.

"I don't know why you need to take so much stuff," said Dan as he watched her arranging clothes on the bed.

"It's easy for you, Mr one-pair-of-shorts-will-do. It's different for a woman," she protested.

"How? It's simple. If you forget something, just buy it while you're there. That way, we're not paying for excess baggage," he explained. "Anyway, you don't see many grass skirts for sale around here."

Sally giggled. "I can just see you in a grass skirt."

The flight was long and tedious. Dan was just a little too tall to sit comfortably.

"Why does it always take longer to get somewhere when you can't wait?" asked Sally.

"It always feels that way when you're in a hurry. That is why the trip home always seems to pass quicker. The mind works at a slower pace and isn't as excited when you are coming back."

"I don't even want to think about that bit, Doctor Psychoanalyst," she chided.

Dan looked at his watch. "Only two hours to go. There's time to watch another movie."

She mumbled something about 'seen enough' and turned to look out of the window at the sea of clouds below them.

Stepping out of the air-conditioned cabin into the warmer climate was like stepping from the fridge into the sauna. The air-conditioned cabin had been warmer than the spring morning they had left behind at Heathrow, but the temperature in Honolulu took their breath away.

"Phew! So that's what they mean by a warm welcome," said Dan.

Sally, shielding her eyes from the intense sunlight, said, "I feel like I've been awake forever."

"If you would like to reset your watches, it's ten thirty local time," smiled the stewardess as they passed. "Enjoy your vacation."

Sally was sure she meant it, but it sounded so hollow. She smiled politely and set off down the stairway.

In a whirlwind of eager anticipation, they passed quickly through the airport, the taxi ride, and the hotel lobby. Within no time, the young couple were in their room looking out over the beautiful, deep blue Pacific. The sun was almost directly overhead, and a warm breeze stirred the curtain. The hills were covered in lush, dark green vegetation, and the white horses of the breaking waves turned silver as they caught the sun.

"Paradise," whispered Sally.

She turned to see Dan, freshly changed out of his jeans and into his shorts. Sally checked him over and laughed. "This is Hawaii, not Bermuda."

"Come on baby. Let's get on down to the beach," replied Dan, trying to put on an American accent.

"Aw Honey, I thought we were in Hawaii, not Texas," she laughed, copying his drawl.

The afternoon was spent finding their way around the hotel complex, the beach, the town and of course, the harbour. Everywhere was bustling yet somehow relaxed. Or perhaps it was Sally that was relaxed. She held Dan's hand as they walked. "Waikiki Beach," she said, looking around.

Since arriving, she had eased into the ambience and absorbed the atmosphere of the island where nothing was hurried. Everybody had things to do but it was OK, it didn't need to be right now. Thoughts drifted through her mind, *"So unlike everything at home; this is going to be my best-ever holiday; nothing will spoil it; it is going to be perfect and this will be one to tell the grandchildren."*

'Marlin Fishing, Snorkelling, Scuba Diving, Whale Watching, Swim with the Dolphins'; the billboards on the quayside advertised all the delights she wanted to sample.

She slowed to read all the signs. "I'll have two of everything," she said. "Well, except for the fishing." But Dan had gone. She found him looking at the surfboards leaning against the shop front.

"Dan, you can't buy one, we'll never get it home," she protested.

"No-no. Just looking. I don't think it will be that different from snowboarding," he explained.

"Only warmer," she smiled and hooked herself onto his arm. "Come on, let's book a boat trip."

The Sea was quite still, apart from a gentle swell that seemed to mimic Sally's mood. Surprisingly, her excitement had been replaced with a peaceful joy that radiated from her. It felt like nothing else mattered any more; just being there, in that place, in that moment, life was complete.

"Mornings like this are usually pretty good. There aren't as many boats out," explained Skipper Bill.

"There!" Someone cried out and twenty-five heads turned starboard.

"They're Humpbacks," said Bill.

Occasional black shadows cut the surface some two hundred metres off to the right of the drifting boat. Sally quickly flicked the pages of her "Whale Identification" booklet as she nodded between the book and the Whales.

"Can we get any closer?" asked an impatient middle-aged tourist.

"Sorry Ma'am. This ain't Disneyland. We have to respect them," came the reply.

The woman scowled.

The whales moved on. Twenty minutes later another pod appeared a little closer this time.

"Look! There!" called Dan, pointing to the left.

A spout gushed into the air and a long, dark body rolled like a wave, ending with a classic T-tail as the whale made a dive for deeper water. Everybody gasped.

"Well, there's something you won't see every day," said Bill.

Sally was flicking the pages again. Then she stopped, took Dan's arm and squeezed.

It didn't matter what species the whales were, what mattered was that she was there and experiencing it first-hand. The emotion within her was overwhelming. Tears filled her eyes. She looked at Dan. There was no need for words. No words could explain the depth of feeling she had right then. Dan put his arm around her and held her close.

"You OK?" he asked.

She nodded vigorously but didn't dare speak in case the emotion overtook her.

Another whale passed close to the port side. This time, only Sally saw it as the rest of the group was looking in the other direction. She made eye contact as the whale passed. But somehow it felt more than just looking at each other. It wasn't just a meeting of eyes. It was as though there was an acknowledgement. A meeting of minds. A connection.

She smiled and felt a deep, spiritual upliftment. It was an 'only for you' moment. Her very own private connection. For that one brief, memorable moment, she felt sure that it was just for her and not to be shared.

"Perfect," she whispered to herself.

For the next hour, whales came and went, sometimes quite close. To most of the group, the novelty had now passed. The cameras had stopped clicking. Whales had become commonplace. The excitement had waned. Everybody in the group was by now highly satisfied, even the impatient tourist had a smile on her face. Sally spent the quieter moments reading the booklet, knowing that Dan would make sure she didn't miss anything.

She sat, face to the sun, eyes closed, absorbing as much as she could from every second. The water lapped the side of the boat and the gentle roll of the waves induced a feeling of perfect calm.

"Heaven."

Sally hung on Dan's arm as they walked away from the quayside.

"Can we do Dolphins tomorrow?" she asked. "Oh sorry, now I'm just being selfish. You should go surfing."

"It's OK. There's plenty of time. If the dolphins make you as happy as the whales, then it's worth it. I've never seen you so happy," he smiled. "I'm almost jealous. I wish I could make you that happy."

Sally skipped along beside him. "Oh, you do. You do. Nobody would do for me what you do." They looked at the billboards. "Are you sure it's ok? Shall we book it now before we leave?" she asked.

Dan said, "Why not. I've enjoyed today. Let's make the most of it while we're on a roll."

And so they booked their next excursion, unaware of how much the next 48 hours would change their lives.

"Hello, Miss. Are you back for more?"

Dan and Sally were boarding the same boat the following morning and Skipper Bill welcomed them aboard. Sally questioned whether they were in the right place.

"Oh, Sorry Bill. We're supposed to be swimming with Dolphins today."

Bill laughed. "That's right miss. Same boat, different day. Different direction this morning," as he offered his hand to help her onto the deck.

The small group on board were a little younger this time. There were four bright-eyed, excited children with almost equally excited parents.

Once underway, Bill caught everyone's attention and delivered a lecture on the right and wrong things to do.

"Ladies and gentlemen, boys and girls," he started. "There are signs around the boat that tell you how to behave, but in case you can't read, I'm going to tell you anyway. Never forget, these are wild animals, not pets. They have a will of their own so we might be unlucky; they could be chasing a shoal of fish ten miles away."

Smiles turned to frowns of disappointment.

Bill cracked a smile, "But I'm sure we'll be just fine. Keep your life jacket on at all times. No jewellery or watches that might scratch them. No sunscreen in the water. No feeding them *anything*."

The children were momentarily quietened. In their eyes, Bill had suddenly taken on the character of Captain Hook. He was obviously well-versed in this response.

"So, what's the main thing we've all got to remember?" he asked.

His young audience remained silent. Their attention hung on his every word. He leaned forward, smiled and winked.

"This is going to be the best day of your lives."

Right on cue, the engines roared and the boat lurched forward towards the open sea. Then he shouted; "Let's have some fun," and the children were immediately transformed into a cheering, excited party of noise.

The water was warm and inviting. Separated into small groups and wearing life jackets, the people bobbed around in the sea like corks, scanning the horizon for signs of life.

A dorsal fin appeared. Sally froze with fear as memories of Jaws filled her thoughts.

"Here they are!" declared Bill.

Within seconds they were surrounded. Sally reached out as the first dolphin passed. Dan dipped his head under the surface and swam around trying to count how many visitors had arrived.

"At least four," he thought to himself.

As he surfaced and exhaled, a dolphin did the same. One broke the surface and stopped face-to-face with Sally.

"Hello," she said, instinctively. The dolphin threw back its head and chirped, almost as though it was laughing. Sally laughed in response. It seemed genuinely happy to be here. She made eye contact and once again her emotions soared. She felt so elated.

Sally spoke to the dolphin "Do you know, there is something magical about close contact with other creatures, especially you guys. You have an aura of joy and exuberance which is contagious. It's like its impossible to be sad when I'm with you... I wonder if this is why parents bring their sick children; maybe we all get boost of happiness."

Sally stretched out a hand and a dolphin obliged by swimming alongside. Her hand stroked the full length of its body as it passed. Still in awe of touching its skin, she left her hand outstretched. The dolphin turned and repeated the move in the other direction.

"Wow! This is incredible," she said to Dan.

They then held hands in an attempt to share the moment, The dolphin slowly came from behind and swam underneath their joined hands, rubbing its back under their arms and then separating their hands with its dorsal fin.

"I never thought you could get so close to wild animals. They're obviously used to this kind of thing," observed Dan.

"Aw, he just likes to be stroked," said Sally as it came close for another pass. It swam between them again and they both stroked its sides.

"How do you know it's a He?" asked Dan. "It might be a girl."

"Naw, only a boy demands this much attention," she joked.

Dan and Sally had drifted away from the main party near the boat. This one Dolphin stayed exclusively with them while the others were treating the children to a similar experience.

Dan floated gently on the swell. Then, silently, the dolphin surfaced beside him and looked him straight in the eye. Talking to it just seemed to be the most natural thing in the world.

"Well, you are a handsome creature, aren't you? It's a pleasure to meet you," he said.

"It's a pleasure to meet you too young man."

Dan heard a voice inside his head. He laughed and called to Sally.

"Hey Sal, this one's talking to me."

Sally laughed and swam over to him. "I wonder what they'd say if they could really talk." She reached out and touched its nose.

"Well, it wouldn't be able to talk, would it?" asked Dan. "It hasn't got vocal cords like us."

"I wouldn't call it 'talking', more... 'connecting'."

Dan was trying to keep things on the right side of logic. He was hearing a voice inside his head and trying to analyse what was happening. He laughed, but the laugh did nothing to relieve his discomfort.

"I think I'm projecting answers that I think it would say if it could talk."

Sally looked quizzical. "What do you mean?"

"Well, it's like I'm imagining a conversation. Sort of, answering myself."

Sally laughed. "Why?"

Dan frowned, still trying to sort his thoughts. "I don't know. It just started happening."

Then it happened again:

"I have already told you; it is connecting."

Dan was shocked. "Did I think that?" he asked himself.

He laughed nervously. He guessed from Sally's reaction that this was all inside his own head.

"Did you hear that?" he asked, although he wasn't sure if any answer was going to be the right one.

"Hear what? I can hear them chirping over there. Is that it?" Sally was trying to help but she was not sure what she was helping with.

"Have you thought any weird thoughts?" Dan was utterly confused.

Sally laughed at him. "I have weird thoughts all the time," she replied.

"No – thoughts that aren't your own. Since we've been swimming," he tried to explain.

Sally shook her head. "I don't know what you mean."

She looked at the dolphin that quietly circled and waited beside her. It lifted its head out of the water and then winked at her. Sally was ecstatic.

"I winked."

Dan heard the voice in his head again.

"Was that coincidence or did he really mean it?" Sally asked.

"Mean what?" Dan asked.

"It winked at me," she grinned.

Dan's mind went into a panic. The questions running through his head were coming so thick and fast he felt like his brain couldn't compute. He was fascinated by this possible 'connection', but that was impossible.

Wasn't it?

His eyes widened, darting from one thing to the next. The Boat. Sally. The dolphin.

His fight-or-flight senses were on high alert. How far was the boat? Could things turn nasty? Is Sally safe? In his panic, he stretched forward and started swimming for the sanctuary of the boat as fast as the restrictive life jacket would allow.

The dolphin swam gently beside him, in silence. Quiet. Sleek. Powerful. Peaceful.

After the first few strokes, Dan began to swim a little slower. Normality seemed to return. The dolphin was quiet and gentle, and somehow caring. A peaceful calm replaced Dan's panic. Sally caught up. Still, the dolphin was silent.

"Are you OK?" asked Sally. "You just shot off like you'd seen a shark or something."

Dan took a few deep breaths and held onto Sally. His brain was still on high alert. He blinked continuously, first looking one way, then the other.

How come it was only happening to him?

Surely Sally would be more receptive to such an idea.

What would she think if he told her the truth?

What would anyone else think?

Why me?

He closed his eyes and tried to regain his breath. "I just need to try something."

Sally was confused. "What? What are you talking about?"

"Sshh," said Dan quietly.

He took another few deep breaths, and once he was composed, he whispered. "OK big boy, prove it," he challenged.

"We connect with everyone that comes. You are the first to respond."

Dan was getting used to this. There was no need to talk. This must be some kind of telepathy, so he thought of his response in his imagination.

"I'm still not convinced; I could have thought that answer myself."

Sally trod water, frowning at her husband as he muttered under his breath. Something was troubling him, and it frightened her. She held onto his arms.

"I winked."

Dan spoke out loud, "I knew that", then he paused to think a little further, "But I didn't see it."

"Knew what? Didn't see what?" asked Sally, her voice rising as she became more uncomfortable. Dan put a calming hand out to her.

"Babe, you're not going to believe this," he started, but knowing Sally as he did, instinctively he knew she would accept all that he was about to say.

A realisation dawned upon him and with it came a calmness and a 'knowing'.

It was as though all this had been planned from the start; his first meeting years ago with Dr Dobbs the dolphin expert, the television programme, the idea of the holiday and how easily everything had fallen into place. This was why they had to come here.

Dan nodded towards the dolphin. "He's talking to me."

"Yeah right. I can't hear anything. Anyway, you said they can't speak," she said drily.

"Be still and listen," he instructed.

Sally listened. After a few seconds of silence, she spoke "Nope. Must just be you then."

"Well, he didn't say anything," Dan explained.

"Course not," said Sally.

He shook his head, totally bewildered.

"We connect with everyone that comes. You are the first to respond."

Sally broke the mood. "Dan. I think I've been treading water too long. I'm getting a cramp."

She tried to massage her calf without sinking. By this time, they had drifted some fifty metres from the boat. Dan was about to try attracting Bill's attention when the dolphin swam up to Sally, winked and then moved close to her side.

"He wants you to hold on to his dorsal and he's going to take you back to the boat," said Dan.

She laughed. "How do you know that?"

"I just do. It's his way of proving that we've connected."

She looked at the dolphin, glanced at the boat and then turned to Dan. "Bill said we shouldn't," she protested.

Dan smiled. "And the dolphin said it's OK. Anyway, what could he do? Throw us overboard?"

As soon as Sally cupped her hand around the front of his dorsal, the dolphin accelerated away, dragging her along. Sally was so surprised that she squealed with delight as they created a bow wave at such speed.

Just as Dan had promised, Sally was delivered safely to the landing stage at the stern of the boat. She took hold of the grab-rail, and the dolphin sank out of sight.

Skipper Bill was the first to speak. "Well, in all my years, I've never seen anything like that. That was a circus trick, not the act of a wild dolphin."

"I got cramp," Sally explained. "He just knew I was in trouble and brought me back."

As she massaged her calf muscle the dolphin returned to Dan and delivered him in exactly the same way. The crew and all the swimmers could only stare at this unbelievable turn of events.

As soon as Dan was safely delivered to the boat, all the dolphins left. Dan spent the next few minutes holding onto the landing stage, trying to make sense of all that had just happened as he got his breath back. He pulled himself out of the water to sit beside his wife. The voice appeared inside his head once again.

"We will connect again very soon young man."

They sat quietly inboard with towels draped over their shoulders while the remains of the group climbed aboard. "Don't say anything to anyone," Dan whispered. "They'll have us locked up."

So they travelled back to the quay in silence, their thoughts flying faster than ever before. Sally whispered a quiet, embarrassed "Thank you" as Bill helped her ashore, but no further words were spoken.

The silence continued all the way along the seafront and back to the hotel, both keeping the secret, yet more than anything wanting to talk it through. They hurried through the hotel lobby and back to their room. Once the door was securely locked, Dan leaned his back against it as if locking the whole world out behind him. At last, it felt safe enough to talk.

"I don't know what to do. I just don't know how to handle it," he started.

"Are you absolutely sure it wasn't just your imagination?" Sally asked.

Dan shook his head. "I've thought about that. It can't have been. I knew he winked at you, but I didn't see it. He told me."

"I told you. I remember telling you," said Sally, searching for an explanation.

"Yes, but I knew before you told me," he explained. "And I knew he wanted to take you back to the boat. That's pretty damned convincing if you think about it. There's no other explanation."

Sally frowned, still searching for sensible answers. Try as they might, no other explanation fit. Still thinking, realisation dawned and she raised her head to look at him. "Oh, my God! You're right. There really is no other explanation. I really do believe you. Wouldn't it be fantastic?"

Dan was more circumspect. "I've been thinking about that too. Remember what Bill said about the circus trick? That's all it would become. We'd be in the spotlight, ridiculed, laughed at." He paused, sighed and then continued. "Not only would we be the standing joke but what about work? How do you think they'd react?" He waved his arm, "I can see it now 'Dr Doolittle Banker Suspended Pending Psychiatric Evaluation'. I'd never work again," he grimaced.

"You might not need to. If we could convince the world, it could be a whole new way of life," Sally suggested.

"I've thought about that too. And what about the dolphin?" Dan looked through the window and out to sea. "I wouldn't want him to be a circus attraction. They'd catch him, imprison him, experiment, God knows what. This could be massive, and I don't honestly know if you, me, or he would cope."

Sally stared into space. "I never thought of it like that. I was only seeing the good."

"Maybe there is some good. I just can't see it yet," Dan sighed. "I'm just so churned up with such a mix of thoughts and emotions. In one sense I'm thrilled and excited, honoured even. Then again, I'm worried, scared of the consequences, frightened of starting something that could get totally out of control. I've got all this confusion."

His anxiety was evident as he paced the floor, unable to keep still.

"Why me? Why not you? Why at all? Then, I suppose, there's a responsibility to do the right thing, to do what's right for the dolphin. I just can't get my head round it all."

He forced a laugh. "I think I need a drink."

They both fell quiet and went out onto the balcony. It was too big an issue for such a small room. They stared out to sea and watched the sunset.

Eventually, Sally broke the silence. "So what happens next?" she asked quietly.

"I don't know. I think we should keep this completely to ourselves," he shrugged. "And maybe just keep away from the ocean."

Sally felt the same anguish and uncertainty.

"We can't just let it go. There could be so many benefits, both for us and them. Breakthroughs like this only happen once every blue moon. We can't miss out on a chance like this."

After another long pause, Dan seemed to find some clarity in the fog.

"It's a big ocean. We may never see him again." He paused. "Right. The odds of finding him again must be thousands to one. So, if it happens, it's happened for a reason, and you're right. I don't think I've got the right to deny that opportunity. So let's play the odds and see what happens."

Sally looked into his eyes and smiled. "You look like you've made a decision."

Dan nodded. "Tomorrow morning we'll go down to the beach, hire a little boat and go out into the bay on our own. We'll take a picnic and spend all day there."

Sally had already started her mental list;

"Masks, snorkels, sunscreen, buy a cool box, maybe take a bottle of wine?"

Dan smiled. "Yes, why not? If he doesn't turn up, then we'll just enjoy the peace of the ocean."

Sally smiled and nodded. "I think he'll turn up."

Dan nodded in return but without smiling said, "I know he will."

They were down at the harbour before most of the holidaymakers were even out of bed.

As the hire kiosk opened, they became the first customer of the day.

They decided to head along the coast towards the airport which would offer some privacy from the more public beaches. This needed to be as private as possible. The little outboard chugged and pushed them around the headland and away from civilisation.

It wasn't long before:

"We are so pleased that you have come to visit us again."

"He's here," Dan exclaimed in a mixture of trepidation and excitement.

Sally scanned around as quickly as she could. "I don't see anything."

A few seconds later a dark shadow rose from the depths to glide alongside the boat.

"Told you."

"How did you know?" asked Sal.

"I've told you. I get a thought in my head that I know isn't mine. It's almost like a conversation with myself. Maybe I'm just turning schizophrenic. What I really don't understand is how come there is no language barrier. He understands my question and I understand his answers. Weird or what?"

"We use the universal connection that all creatures have; it's just that humans have lost their ability to use it."

"How do you mean?" asked Dan, out loud. Sally looked up but realised the question wasn't for her.

"There is no need to voice your question. I feel your intention and understand your emotion. When you hear me, it is your own voice you hear. This is your mind's way of receiving my intention and my emotion."

Dan laughed. "That explains why you're so good at English."

"Language is no barrier to this connection."

Dan experimented with his thoughts. "What do you mean 'all creatures have this connection'?"

The dolphin's answer came into his mind almost before he had formed the question.

"You wonder how we find each other in miles of open ocean. You wonder how birds all leave the wire at once to migrate. You wonder why all prey animals move as one when they are threatened. You wonder how animals pass information to their babies. All this is the connection. An unseen connection that runs through all creation."

Dan turned to Sally. "Wow! This is profound. I think we'd better start writing it down."

"Committing our communication to paper will not be necessary. All that we share will stay with you undimmed. That is the way with the connection."

This was surreal, unbelievable. Dan slowly shook his head. "This could blow my mind."

"No. Your mind can cope with this. It is natural. You are using a part of your brain that has been dormant in humans for many years."

A frown of curiosity grew across Dan's face. "Hang on. How come you know about birds? And lions? And paper? This can't be right!"

"How we know these things will become obvious to you as you gain a deeper understanding, but I will help. If my mind is connected to yours, then all your knowledge is shared. This way we know about your world and your activities."

"So how come I can't read your mind? This should work both ways."

"We are more practised than you are. You may develop the skill, but it takes time and training."

Dan's mind began to race ahead. Myriad thoughts fought for his attention, flashing and crowding through in rapid succession; questions, answers, realisation.

"We may also teach control. To achieve clarity, measured deliberation must be employed."

"Jeez. Well, *that* certainly didn't come from my mind."

Sally asked, "What's that?"

"To achieve clarity, measured deliberation must be employed."

Sally was impressed. "Wow! 'Daniel the philosopher' all of a sudden. I hope you're going to share all this."

Dan offered no answer. Once again he looked deep in thought.

"So where is all this going to lead? What purpose is there to it?"

"We share your concerns. Thank you for considering the consequences. However, although humans believe they have

ultimate control, you must understand that where nature is concerned this is not so. Only human arrogance can see it this way."

"There's no need to be offensive," Dan said defensively.

"Allow me to explain. Since life began there has been a connection between all life on Earth. For thousands of years, we had very little contact with your species. You were on the land, and we were in the sea. We knew of each other's existence and the connection was still there; think of all the Maori art that depicts sea creatures. Sadly, the connection grew weaker over time and when you started to develop your technologies the link was lost.

Mankind became more than the animal he was as he separated himself from nature.

From that time on we have strived to connect.

Whenever a human comes into contact with nature, if he is sensitive, he still feels the connection. It is something deep inside. Like the inner peace you feel when you walk in the countryside. Or the peace you feel sitting beneath a tree on a summer's day.

You know it firstly with your own kind. When you see the wet eyes of a needy child you feel compassion and the urge to help.

This should continue into the natural world beyond humankind, perhaps when you see a baby chimpanzee, or maybe when you get to know your new pet puppy.

It is the one-ness. The connection with nature. The connection with life. This, my friend, is the connection."

"Like when you make eye contact with a dolphin."

"Precisely. And this is the reason that many of your fellow humans feel a healing when they connect with dolphins."

Dan relaxed into a feeling of complete contentment. All his anxieties faded away. Happiness seemed to swell his heart as he absorbed the atmosphere and absorbed the knowledge. He felt that he had the connection, not only with the dolphin but with all of life, as though his senses had reached out and connected with everything there was. It was overwhelming. He was perfectly still, yet sharply aware of everything; the warmth and light of the sun, the gentle rocking of the boat on the sea, the closeness of Sally and the dolphin. In that moment life was perfect.

He opened his eyes to see Sally. She had her hand to her mouth and tears welled in her eyes. "Oh, my God. I've got it too," she cried.

Dan put his arms around her and they lay in the bottom of the boat.

The dolphin was still there but he remained respectfully silent while the connection and the emotion washed through and over them both.

After a while, Sally spoke. "I think you have much to teach us," said Sally.

"Alas, no. In knowledge and intelligence, the dolphin cannot compete."

"But you know much that we don't, about nature and things?" she asked.

"We have been hoping for a connection that we may be able to open the eyes and the minds of mankind, to express our fears for the Earth, for nature and for you, our fellow beings."

The mood changed. "Fears for us?" Sally asked.

"We feel this in the connections we make every day with your swimmers. Much of the disease around you is brought

about by yourselves. You suffer more disease than ever before, yet you choose to ignore the causes.

You have now developed so many drugs – for medicine or other uses. And others such as alcohol and caffeine, even sugar and chocolate. An organic body was never intended to cope with such excesses. Over-development brings over-indulgence, and with the excesses, there are ever greater strains on the body. The human body evolved for movement and agility. Less exercise and more food puts a greater strain on muscles and organs. Higher sugar intake needs to be burned off, but your lifestyle does not permit this. You treat your machines much better than you treat yourselves.

You must also be careful of the way you have harnessed nature. We use what you would call the Earth's magnetic field in a natural way to know where we are. Many humans feel an inbuilt compass to find their way around in a way very similar to ours, in that they automatically know which way to travel. So imagine how this sense is disrupted when it is subject to the magnetic fields created by electrically powered machinery or even battery-powered gadgets such as your computers and cell phones. You are surrounding yourselves with these unnatural magnetic fields that the body has not evolved to cope with. The consequence of this is that the cells in the body react adversely to the disturbance of their natural rhythm and balance. Mankind has tamed and harnessed what you call electricity way beyond what nature intended."

"So our excesses will be our downfall," observed Dan. He tried throwing in some defence for the future. "We've known this for a long time. It hasn't made a difference at all. Lifespan is still increasing."

"This is falsely prolonged by your drugs. Eventually, the cells of the natural framework will begin to disintegrate. Is it not true that you are seeing greater numbers of different cancers and other diseases for which you have no cure? There comes a time when the fabric of the body can no longer hold itself together under the constant attack of unnatural substances."

"I'm so glad I don't smoke," said Sally, almost under her breath. She could tell that the dolphin understood. She still felt its compassion, sympathy and love.

"We'll just have to swim more and eat lots of fish," she added.

"What? Everybody in the world?" asked Dan.

The dolphin raised its head above the surface and looked at them. They both felt the sympathy turn into a plea.

"The forest has been consumed. The land has been raped. The Earth has been scarred and made to give up her treasures. What is to become of the sea? Before your technology, there was a deeper understanding. The connection was still strong. Some of your original native tribes still feel this but it weakens with every generation.

The indigenous people of the North American continent have a poem which your world would do well to take heed of. I should like to quote it for you. Remember it well, as I know you will."

There was a moment's pause, as if the dolphin was trying to remember.

"Only when the last tree has died,
and the last river has been poisoned,

*and the last fish has been caught
will we realise that we cannot eat money."*

"So, are you telling us that the human race is going to burn itself out?" asked Dan.

"Examine the evidence. Think for yourselves. We feel compassion and pity for the human burnout."

Dan felt that he was now on the same wavelength as the dolphin and his statements started to sound as though the dolphin himself had voiced them. "We take all that we can from the land until it can no longer support us, so we use our technology to create false landscapes with intensive farming techniques. But we are producing children faster than we are producing food. We dig bigger holes to extract fewer minerals and bleed the earth dry of its resources, yet we miss the obvious. We are the locusts on the face of the Earth."

He turned to the dolphin, his voice saddened with the realisation. He somehow felt personally responsible.

"Your reference to the locust is very apt. Are you aware of what happens to a mass locust infestation?"

"Yes – it was awful, devastating. All that destruction, and no crops left for all those poor starving children," said Sally.

"What happened to the locusts?"

Dan explained, "Well, fortunately, they died out. Too many of them and not enough food. They ate themselves out, so they starved. Good job too."

"This is the balance of nature. Feast and famine. Food and starvation, then the balance is restored. This is the way of things on Earth. Nature will always restore the balance."

There was a pause for the realisation to sink in.

"If you view a city from high in the air, what do you see?"

"Thousands of people scurrying about like ants," observed Sally. "Roads are like arteries and cars are like blood vessels all flowing along."

"Can you see the connection? The Earth will look after itself. Nature will take its course and balance will be restored."

Dan spoke quietly. "Feast and Famine. Starvation will lead to riots. It will lead to war and a global meltdown."

Sally held on to him.

"But what can we do? Two insignificant people amongst so many millions," pleaded Sally. She absent-mindedly trailed her hand in the water. The dolphin brushed past gently as if to offer reassurance.

"The catastrophe you foresee may not happen; other things are beginning to move."

"Such as?" Dan asked. The voice continued, just as measured and just as clear as it had begun.

"There is a growing realisation amongst the enlightened few. If this can be sustained, nurtured and widened, then there is hope."

"I don't think you realise the size of it. There are seven billion people on Earth now," Dan explained.

"And most of them are so bloody selfish that they would ignore us anyway," added Sally.

"Locusts indeed. We are aware of the problem. This is why we need to connect with more of your kind. Mankind believes that they have evolved beyond their origins, yet they still display so many animal traits. Yes, there are some that have grown, and we see that they despair of their brethren. We see examples of greed, aggression and selfishness in one

man, but then altruism and love in the next. It is all part of the progress along the path you are on. If your more enlightened side could grow, mankind could truly become the superior being he yearns to be."

"But there has always been selfishness and greed," observed Dan.

"It is inherent in the nature of man to be greedy. We see this in our connections, but at the point of extreme need, greed is surpassed by altruism; a drowning man will always try to help a drowning child. This shows us that there is hope.

You should witness more of this altruism with each generation; the type of man that feels a greater satisfaction from helping his neighbour, rather than charging a fee for his time."

Dan felt a pang of guilt. Sally interjected, "Well, there are examples of this, but sadly not enough."

The mood in the boat had now changed completely. The connection and the feeling of love were still as strong, but the emotion now felt like a bereavement.

Silence prevailed as they were both lost in deep thought. The dolphin respected their silence.

Eventually, Dan spoke, slowly and deliberately and out loud in a measure to formulate his own thoughts and allow Sally to hear.

"The Politicians won't listen. Businessmen certainly won't listen. All the decision-makers of the world simply won't be interested. They'll all want an angle, if things don't fit into their own agenda, they will not listen. This will not matter to anyone unless they feel that it is personal. If it affects them personally, then attitudes will change but unless we can make them see that, we'll have no chance."

"This is a human characteristic that we would expect. The smoker continues in the blind belief that they are immune, refusing to accept the evidence. Then when they become ill, they become evangelical converts."

Sally spoke. "OK, you've been clever enough to forewarn us of the fall. Are you wise enough to offer us a solution?"

Dan looked surprised. "That was a bit forthright," he said indignantly as if defending the dolphin. Sally shrugged, "I can't see a way out. Maybe he can," she explained.

"Your greatest religion started with the ideas of one man. This gives us hope that an idea can multiply in the minds of mankind."

Dan answered, "Well, yes it can. But that could take a thousand years. The way you talk we don't have that sort of time. Something must be done now. We cannot continue as we are. But the task is massive. Converting two people in a boat is not going to change the world. A 'mass connection' would help. Is that possible?"

Sally answered first. "Even if every enlightened human being on the planet connected, it still wouldn't be enough. We'd just be ridiculed as cranky tree-huggers."

"Let's just sit still," Dan suggested. "Let the day wash over us and see if any ideas emerge."

Sally raised her eyebrows. "I quite like this new Daniel the philosopher."

"Then let's hope he has a brainwave," answered Dan.

Silence fell once more. The waves gently rocked the boat, and the sun gradually rose in the sky while the dolphin slowly circled the boat. Quietly unobtrusive, but there, radiating love and compassion and patience.

The silence created one of those periods where minutes passed like hours, or maybe it was the opposite. It was impossible to know how long it lasted.

Eventually, Sally challenged the dolphin again. She asked in her mind, "Any ideas?"

"We transmit a message to our neighbours, who repeat it to theirs. By this process, we can reach all of our family in seconds, and all others within the day. Perhaps you could use your media to the same effect."

"If only human communication could be so simple. I suppose if you have a bad thought your neighbours pick it up straight away. If humans were that connected and transparent, it would change the way we behave, and it would certainly upset a lot of people I know," Dan observed.

Sally offered, "TV, YouTube, Facebook, a website, maybe even write a book?"

"Hm. How successful do you think that would be?" asked Dan. "It's almost impossible to get that level of exposure, and even if we get the exposure, how many people would actually be prepared to change their lives? I think we should read Dr Dobbs' books again first."

"Who?"

"The dolphin expert I told you about. I think he was probably in this exact position years ago."

"And maybe he's been having this same battle for years," observed Sally.

"You can only be responsible for your own actions. Will you actually change your own lives?"

"I, I, I hadn't even thought that far," answered Sally.

"And therein lies the problem. We are still a part of that very problem," added Dan. "All I can seem to think of are clichés; 'The longest journey starts with the smallest step', 'So long as you keep putting one foot in front of the other, you are bound to reach your destination'."

Sally joined in "Constant dripping wears away a stone."

"I suppose in this context they are all accurate, but I'm starting to think about our own situation. How can we preach to the world unless we change our own lifestyle? You must walk the walk or you don't have any credibility," Dan explained.

"Or any conviction," added Sally. "You do realise how far this has to go?" she asked.

"Sell the car and buy a bicycle," Dan offered.

"Sell the house and live in a tent," she retorted.

"Is it actually possible to live in the modern world without the resources?"

Sally looked for the dolphin.

"Bottom line? I suppose all we need is food and shelter. Everything else is just comfort."

"Hm, so what you're asking is to throw away everything we've achieved since the Bronze Age," said Dan.

"No, I don't think so," answered Sally "Just utilise different technology that doesn't cost the earth."

Dan raised his eyebrows. "Oh, very sharp! Sharp, but accurate."

They fell into silence and waited for the dolphin to communicate.

After a few more minutes of silence, they began to feel alone and vulnerable in a wide-open ocean.

"He's gone," said Dan.

"Disconnected," said Sally. They waited in silence and hope for a few more minutes but the ocean remained vast and empty.

An aeroplane passed over, losing height as it brought yet more holidaymakers into the airport.

"Isn't that odd?" Dan noted. "They've probably been passing over every few minutes all day and we never even noticed."

Sally watched the plane land and then turned to Dan. "So now what do we do?"

Dan pulled on the starter and pointed the boat back towards the harbour. He paused for a moment then said, "We could pretend it never happened," he offered.

"Don't you think that's a bit irresponsible?"

"I said we 'could', I didn't say we should."

Sally looked relieved and lay with her head on his thigh. "I'd like to bring our child into a better world, not a dying one."

Dan's eyes widened, "Child?"

Sally smiled. "I know the timing's not great, but I think I'm pregnant."

Dan let go of the tiller and pulled her close, placing his hand on her stomach.

"That's it then. No excuses. No going back. We've got to do it for him."

"Her," she corrected.

Ten miles away, the dolphin rejoined his pod in search of the next shoal of fish.

It was hard to believe that five years passed so quickly, the afternoon sun shone brightly, but most of its warmth was taken by the breeze. An old, grey tractor chugged slowly along the lane past the cottage. Its driver raised his arm in an idle wave to the couple sitting in the garden. They smiled and returned the wave. Dan then raised his binoculars and looked out to sea, still hoping to catch a ripple in the waves which carried the hope of cetacean life.

County Clare has its own residential dolphin population. Occasionally, they still made connections, but the dolphins here weren't as enthusiastic as the ones in the Pacific. Sally thought it was because humans don't like swimming in colder water so there was less interaction. Dan preferred his own theory that they had given us up as a lost cause.

"Wrong time of year," said Sally.

"They're supposed to be here all year round." But they both knew that already.

"Yes, but the fish aren't," she explained.

He put down his binoculars and picked up his laptop. He had just heard the ping of notification that another email had landed.

"Anything interesting?"

Dan glanced at his laptop. "That's different. It seems we have a sympathetic TV researcher. She wants to come and interview us."

"That's up to you," said Sally.

"We have to keep trying. One day the tide will turn," he said, optimistically.

"I don't think it will happen in our lifetime," she replied.

He looked a little saddened as he picked up his binoculars again.

"You okay?" she asked, putting her hand on his shoulder.

He patted her hand. "Wouldn't change a thing," he smiled.

"Are you sure?"

"100%. I wouldn't go back to our old lifestyle for anything. Who cares if no one believes us? We know the truth. And that's all that matters to me."

"Well, I must agree with that one. It's time to go; I have to meet Connor."

"I'll go. It'll make a change for Daddy to meet him from school."

Connor was four years old already. So much had happened yet nothing much had changed. Kilbaha was such a beautiful place. It overlooked the sea and enjoyed a mild climate due to the gulf stream. Life was slow. And it was just about far enough away from civilisation that the only people going there had to have a good reason to go.

Nothing was hurried. Emails can wait, they don't need to be answered immediately. Money was tight but they still had some savings left from the sale of the house. Sally's part-time job provided enough income when there's nothing you really need.

Dan's days were spent writing articles for magazines or offering online support and encouragement to those that found their website. Just occasionally, sympathetic donations arrived. Despite his own lack of progress, he refused to discourage people that had recently undergone a similar life-changing experience, so he had long since stopped offering words of warning about his own experience of ridicule and rejection.

The coffee shop in Kilrush was the chosen venue; quiet, discreet, and anonymous. A woman of indeterminate age walked in. Her smile was warm and her greeting polite. They sat in the corner, just Dan and his latest hope for more serious media exposure.

"I'm so pleased to meet you. I'm Siobhan. As I said in my email, we are doing a series on communication with animals, so when I read about your experience, I just had to meet you."

She seemed serious, asking lots of pre-prepared questions, and talked about TV crews, swimming with dolphins, and her own experience with her pet Labradors. Dan's hopes were raised. Feeling that he was with someone to trust, he relaxed and opened up, answering her questions eagerly and feeding off her compliments.

"Maybe this time..." he thought.

An hour later, his information was exhausted. Siobhan had listened intently and taken pages of notes. They moved to leave.

"So, what happens next?" he asked.

"I take this back to the office, we have a big meeting to discuss whether we have enough content... then I'll let you know."

They never heard from her again.

Connor came running through the gate. "Mummy, Mummy, I painted you at school today," he called, holding his prized picture aloft.

"Oh, darling, thank you." Sally added it to the others that decorated the fridge.

Meanwhile, in the waters off Key West, Florida, a 10-year-old boy swam excitedly towards his mother.

"Mummy, Mummy! The dolphin is talking to me."

His mother smiled and said, "Yes dear. Of course he is. Now come along, it's time to go."

Made in the USA
Monee, IL
03 May 2026

49437832R00030